D1061008

TONK and TONKA

TONK and TONKA

by Eugene Ackerman

ILLUSTRATED BY CARL BURGER

E. P. DUTTON & COMPANY, INC. ⋎ NEW YORK

CLARKE, IRWIN & COMPANY LIMITED ⋎ TORONTO ⋎ VANCOUVER

J
c.2

Text copyright, ©, 1962 by F. Eugene Ackerman
Illustrations copyright, ©, 1962 by E. P. Dutton & Co., Inc.
All rights reserved. Printed in the U.S.A.

FIRST EDITION

No part of this book may be reproduced in any form
without permission in writing from the publisher,
except by a reviewer who wishes to quote brief
passages in connection with a review written for
inclusion in a magazine, newspaper or broadcast.

Published simultaneously in the United States by
E. P. Dutton & Co., Inc., New York, and in Canada
by Clarke, Irwin & Company Limited, Toronto and
Vancouver.

Library of Congress Catalog Card Number: 62-7494

C L NOV 2 2 '68

For Lynwood and Juliana with love

Author's Note

THE story of Tonk and Tonka is based on an actual event. In September, 1955, the Vineyard *Gazette* reported that a pair of wild geese had rushed a hawk that was making a strike upon a Muscovy duck which the geese had adopted. One of the geese killed the hawk with its strong wing.

TONK and TONKA

IT WAS the first week in September. Tonk and Tonka squatted at rest upon the cold, frost-tipped moss. With low quacks of contentment they watched the other blue geese fly in from the north to join them. The blue geese were coming from their nesting grounds scattered over five thousand miles of land and sea along the northern fringes of Baffin Island. They were lighting upon the chill waters of James Bay, a pendant-shaped inlet at the southern tip of mighty Hudson Bay. After

a few days' rest they would resume their long journey southward to their winter homes along the Gulf of Mexico.

The blue geese had arrived on Baffin Island in early June after a long and dangerous flight. They had come to the bleak, fog-swept tundra to build their nests and to hatch their young. No one knows why the blue geese spend the summer in this harsh part of the world. Even the Eskimos avoid it.

During the few months of summer that the geese are nesting, there is no night. It is the time of year when this frozen land is closest to the sun. The sun shines day and night. Its warmth melts the surface frost to a depth of five to ten inches. Sleeping roots and frozen seeds sprout to life from their shal-

low bed. The earth is quickly covered with lichen, ferns, moss, and plants bearing pale flowers. Willowlike vines trail over the ground, and in this bed of down and moss the geese build their nests.

The blue geese are but part of the mighty annual migration of wild life to the Arctic regions. There are also crying loons, wide-winged cranes and swans. The arctic fox, the ermine, and the wolf come to prey upon the birds and their young. The seas are alive with schools of whales, with seals, and the long-tusked walrus and the narwhal. The polar bear prowls the ice floes, softening in the sun. The newly warmed land is full of life, and everywhere there is a sense of hurry, for the time the birds and animals have here is short.

Soon the long arctic night of winter will set in again. Then the tumult of living creatures is stilled. The animals and birds flee the darkening world with their young and begin their migration south. The ice-riven land broods in black silence until the next spring.

Tonk and Tonka are a part of this migration. They had glided down on James Bay the day before. During the summer they had hatched four goslings. Two had been eaten by a hungry arctic fox. Only two were left at the end of the

short summer when Tonk, rising swiftly into the air, honked loudly as a signal that Tonka and the fledglings were to follow him to join the ragged line of geese flying south. Tonka flew easily alongside her mate. The young geese flew uncertainly.

Tonk and Tonka had been mates for three years, and they would remain mates until one of them died. They had hatched their young each summer, and taught them where the berries, shrubs, and bulb-rooted moss could be found. They taught the goslings to fly, and kept them warm under their great wings. Now there was no nest to which the young could return. And once the flight south began, the goslings would have to look out for themselves. Soon they would grow their adult coats of feathers and seek their own mates.

Suddenly the restless geese were quiet. This was their signal. Tonk and Tonka rose on their purple, webbed feet and stretched their wings to the utmost. A majestic goose soared aloft, honking loudly. He was almost three feet long from his outstretched neck to his tail, and his wings were four feet long from tip to tip. With answering honks, excited quacks, and happy barking sounds, the flock of geese rose to follow their leader.

In the confusion of flapping wings and darting bodies it seemed as though the geese would crash into one another. But they quickly straightened into uneven lines of about seventy-five to one hundred geese. Flock after flock, each led by a single goose, rose into the air. The mass flight to the Gulf of Mexico had begun. The flocks would keep closely together on the long journey across middle Canada, down the Mississippi River Valley to Louisiana. There they would come to rest on Vermilion Bay off the Gulf of Mexico, to range up and down the coast until it was time for them to return north.

Flying at a speed of fifty to sixty miles an hour, the blue

geese could make the trip from Canada to Louisiana in two or
three weeks if they did not stop. But, needing rest and food,
they stop often along the way and it is usually about eight
weeks after they leave James Bay that they reach their des-
tination.

As the flock of which Tonk and Tonka were a part fell
into its changing pattern of flight, the leader honked loudly.
The honks were taken up and repeated back along the line.
These calls keep the flock together and warn it of winds or
rain ahead. Mingled with the bell-like honks were the shriller
notes of the goslings who, on their first flight south, mimicked

14

the adult birds. The geese flew higher and higher until they were four to five thousand feet in the air. Beneath them the land was hidden by the clouds. Above them the new morning sun gleamed like live gold in a sky of clear blue.

Then out of the east roared a gleaming silver giant. It was a four-engine turbo prop bound for New York. Instinct warned the leader of the flock that here was a new and terrible danger. At once he led the geese downward. The white heads and rose and pink bills of the adult birds shone in the sun; their long necks were stretched to the utmost. Their great wings swept them to within a thousand feet of the earth. The leading goose honked once more. The airplane was now a shadow disappearing into the sky. The geese turned upward.

Day after day, with a rest every twenty-four hours or so, the birds flew across Canada, past Quebec, toward the Great Lakes and the Mississippi Valley. In the stillness of the night, farmers taking a last look at their livestock in fields and barns, heard high above them a blare of honks. And if the night was clear, cold, and silent, they could even hear the rush of wings. Winter was coming. The geese were on the wing, going south.

II

THREE weeks had passed since Tonk and Tonka had taken off from James Bay. Now the trees were red and yellow and orange in the autumn haze. Below them gleamed the hurrying waters of the Mississippi River.

Almost without warning, out from the south and west came strong, screaming winds. The geese flew higher and higher to avoid them. The winds were part of a series of violent storms roaring up from Texas and down from western Canada, which joined forces as they swept across the Great

Plains. In their fury they left ruin and death. Rivers ran wide in floods. Houses were blown over. Then, as the storms were about to quiet down, a hurricane called Mathilda, which had begun its course north from the Caribbean Sea weeks before, joined the wild gales from the west and spurred them on to new destruction.

The winds blew the geese farther and farther eastward, beating at their tired wings until, in exhaustion, hundreds of birds fell heavily to earth.

Tonk and Tonka had managed to stay close together. Then, toward the dawn of one long dark night a final burst

of wind caught them, hurled them aloft, and threw them downward. For a while Tonk was tumbled over and over, but at last his powerful wings held him steady and he glided toward the ground. Below him he saw Tonka. One of her wings was beating slowly, the other drooped idly. She was falling down, down. Only her outstretched wing kept her from dropping like a rock. The wind died suddenly. With a thrust of his wings, Tonk flew alongside his mate. Tonka quacked gently. In reply Tonk honked hoarsely over and over again. He was urging her to fly upward. She was telling him that she was hurt; she could not fly, and she was frightened.

As they came to the land, Tonka slumped over and rolled sidewise. But she got to her feet. Tonk alighted proudly, his pink legs and purple-webbed feet thrust forward. The geese had reached Queen's Island, off the Massachusetts coast, more than a thousand miles east of their regular flying course.

Tonk and Tonka did not land on the lagoons or marshes that cut up the island into little pockets of protection and food for wildlife. They were on a narrow dirt road that lay between two stone walls. The storm had littered the road with branches, piling them up against the walls. Tonk and Tonka crept wearily under a branch. Leaning together they folded their long necks against their breasts and slept in exhaustion.

The bright sunlight and the sound of excited quacks aroused them. The strange sounds bewildered them. They were familiar but at the same time different from the sounds they knew. What Tonk and Tonka were hearing were the quacks of Muscovy ducks, those queer, good-natured birds that look like clowns and are fond of people.

Tonk and Tonka heard other sounds such as they had never heard before. A little girl, just past five, was laughing and talking to her father as she watched her ten-year-old brother sprinkle cracked corn on the ground. It was snatched up at once by a solemn line of Muscovy ducks. Tonk and Tonka had seen human beings before, but only at a distance when they were resting between flights. Their fear of people was part of the instinctive wariness of wild creatures who keep to themselves and trust only nature.

Tonk's first impulse was to fly to the freedom and safety of the sky. He settled back on his webbed feet and spread his wings. Then he saw Tonka quacking in pain. She could lift only one wing. Dropping his wings he stood erect and with arched neck, walked slowly forward beside his injured mate like a soldier on parade. Emmy saw them first.

"Daddy!" she cried. "Look, Daddy! Geese, beautiful geese. And one of them is hurt."

Her father shook his head in surprise. "They must have been blown down by the storm along with our chimney and the branches of the trees."

Her brother Bill tossed a handful of cracked corn before Tonk and Tonka. Slowly, and with the dignity of an honored guest, Tonk bent his neck and nibbled uncertainly. Tonka promptly followed his example. Then they both began to eat as though they were starved — as indeed they were.

The ducks, who had stood silently by, too surprised even to quack, now began to move about uneasily. Then the drake, with puffed-out breast, strutted forward and quacked amiably. Immediately his mate bustled after him, followed by the other ducks. Tonk and Tonka regarded them gravely; then they quacked back.

Bill soon ran out of corn and raced back to the yellow-and-white barn for more. "And bring some water," his father called after him.

Mr. Hopkins moved closer to Tonka to look at her drooping wing. He could not judge whether it was broken or whether it had just been pulled out of joint. If it was out of

joint, he thought that he could fix it. But if Tonka had broken her wing, her case was hopeless. The bone of a wild goose's wing is like steel, strong and flexible, so that it can hurl the goose's seven- to ten- to fifteen-pound weight at a speed of fifty miles an hour and more, day after day.

While he was puzzling over his plan of action, Bill came hurrying back with the can of corn, followed by his mother carrying a bowl of water.

"What beautiful geese!" Mrs. Hopkins exclaimed. "Oh, and one has a badly hurt wing." Her husband nodded.

"Yes, and the problem is how to fix it," he said.

Tonk and Tonka lost no time pecking at the corn and drinking from the bowl. In drinking they opened their bills, put the lower half under the water like a spoon, and lifting their heads slowly let the water trickle down their long necks.

"Geese like these are rare around here," Mr. Hopkins explained. "They are of the genus *Chen*. There are about two hundred species throughout the world. About fifty kinds are found in North America. They have many names — blue snow goose, blue winged goose, blue brant. . . . " He paused. Bill and Emmy were not listening. Their attention was entirely on forlorn Tonka.

"Don't worry," he told the children. "Its mate won't desert it." He turned to Mrs. Hopkins. "I wonder if I can fix that wing, and how I can go about it."

"Why not feed the geese some of that sleeping medicine the vet gave you for Micky when he had those thorns in his paws," she said. "It put him to sleep. If it worked on a dog it might very well work on a goose."

"Bill," she called. "Start walking slowly up the lane, tossing the corn as you go."

"Emmy, take the bowl of water and go along with Bill. The geese are half starved. I'm sure they will follow you."

Bill and Emmy walked slowly up the lane. Tonk and Tonka, after a moment, followed, pecking at the driblets of corn that Bill scattered.

The lane curved to the right. Around the curve was a low white house in a big yard. To the left was the duck yard surrounded by a wire fence six feet high, just high enough to keep any venturesome Muscovy duck with clipped wings from trying to fly over it.

Mr. and Mrs. Hopkins watched anxiously as Bill turned in at the open wire gate of the duck enclosure. For an instant Tonk and Tonka stopped; then they walked in. Tonk led the

way to a shaded spot under a low bush. There he squatted down with Tonka. They folded their long necks against their breasts and closed their eyes.

"Poor things," Mrs. Hopkins whispered. "They're worn out. Now Emmy, give Daddy the bowl of water."

"He will fix the goose's wing, won't he?" she asked.

Her mother nodded assurance. Her father went to the barn adjoining the duck enclosure. He took a bottle from the shelf, poured half the liquid into the bowl from which the geese had been drinking, added more water, and then filled the bowl with cracked corn.

III

TONK and Tonka were so tired they were barely able to raise their heads when Mr. Hopkins and Bill gave them the corn and the water dosed with the sleeping medicine. The Muscovy ducks crowded around as though the corn and water were intended for them as well.

"Chase them away or we'll have a colony of sleeping ducks," Mr. Hopkins told Bill.

Tonk and Tonka were still hungry. They began to peck

at the corn and to drink from the bowl. Bill and his father made several quiet visits to the duckyard. The first two times they found the geese still eating. The third time Tonk and Tonka were squatting close together, heads tucked in and eyes closed. It was twilight when father and son made their fourth visit. Bill gave a shout.

Tonka was rolling over sidewise on the uninjured wing. A moment later Tonk toppled slowly. Both lay motionless on their sides. Mr. Hopkins gently poked Tonka. She did not move. He felt around and under the wing. And then with expert hands he carefully pulled and twisted the wing, and let it fall back. Tonka quacked uneasily and stirred, but she did not waken.

"Bill, it's not broken, just pulled out of joint," Mr. Hopkins said with relief. "I put it back. I believe it will be as good as new."

Tonk and Tonka did not waken until the following morning. Tonk rose unsteadily to his feet and honked in alarm as he saw Tonka lying on her side. His repeated honks wakened her and she scrambled upright.

As the days passed it appeared certain that the wing was healing. Tonka stretched it a little more each day, letting it

fall against her side where it lay snugly. The geese became more at home in the duckyard, and on the dirt road where the children paraded them after school. They shared the food of the Muscovy ducks, feeding among their smaller friends with a quiet, unhurried dignity.

Mr. Hopkins warned his family that Tonk and Tonka would fly away as soon as Tonka's wing was healed. But Emmy and Bill were sure that the geese would like the duckyard so well that they would settle down there to hatch a family. But their mother told them, "The geese belong to no one. They are creatures of the sky. They will go back there some day."

Fall deepened into winter and still Tonka had not taken wing. Tonk had long since gone on short flights by himself, landing on Tisman Pond, where he rode the small waves. There he pecked at the grasses that grew on the shallow bottom of the pond, upending his brightly colored body until he looked like a gay balloon drifting in the water. He always came up chewing something with his saw-edged bill. He would repeat this performance for hours on end.

One day in February, just after Tonk had spread his wings and soared into the air, Tonka followed him.

"Look!" called Mrs. Hopkins. "The wing is well again. There go our geese. Goodbye, God speed you."

Bill felt tears coming to his eyes, and turned away to hide them. The Muscovy ducks began quacking loudly, as though they too were saying goodbye to their friends. Emmy pulled at her father's sleeve, and said confidently: "You'll get them to come back again, won't you, Daddy?"

Her father tried to reassure her but he knew that the geese must leave them someday. This might be the time.

But their fears and farewells were not needed. As the evening shadows deepened, honks were heard over the duck-yard, and two great birds, with blue-gray wings, spiraled slowly down.

Tonk and Tonka had come back.

The hurricane that had swept Tonk and Tonka onto Queen's Island had also driven down other birds. Among them was a pair of hawks blown northward from the pine forests of Virginia.

Hawks belong to the family of fierce, flesh-eating birds that includes the buzzard, the kite, the falcon, and more than two hundred other birds that feed on small animals and birds they overcome and carry away. They are the hunters of the air, cruising about in the skies, ready to pounce with their long curved talons on their victims. Young chickens, geese, robins, finches, scarlet tanagers, scurrying grouse, field mice, and chipmunks are all their prey, as well as rats and other rodents. The hawks catch their victims in the air or snatch them from the ground. They are part of nature's plan to control the size of the bird population, which in the United States and Canada alone numbers many billions.

The pair of hawks blown onto Queen's Island were goshawks, among the largest and most powerful birds of prey. Goshawks make their homes in the northern parts of the United States and in southern Canada, where they sally forth to hunt from a cover of trees and bushes. Their bodies of bluish feathers with white breast and black head are about two feet long, and they have a wingspread of nearly four feet. A black stripe under each eye gives the goshawk the look of a flying pirate. They are quick and bold, and will

33

swoop down into a barnyard to snatch a fowl right under its owner's eyes.

On Queen's Island the goshawks found a stony ledge on the rock cliffs that overlooked the sea. There they built their nest of sticks and leaves, and settled down to spend the winter. Goshawks gorge themselves once every two or three days, except when they are hatching and raising their young, and then they are always hungry. They dash about the skies or skim down to earth, killing any moving creature that they can carry home.

It was in April, the usual hatching time, that the female hawk laid her first egg. Within a week she laid three more. As she sat on the nest, her mate flew about searching for food. One morning the hawk flew over the Hopkins' yard and sighted the Muscovy ducks waddling down the lane behind Bill. Tonk and Tonka, sleek and calm, followed behind. There were ten new ducklings now, hatched just three weeks before. Their mother waddled proudly, fat stomach pushed out, quacking to the puffs of feathers and hungry bills that stumbled about her.

The attack came so fast that it was almost over before Bill was aware of it. The hawk, with thick outspread legs and

35

talons, swooped down. Only the mother duck sensed its approach. With fluttering movements she threw herself against the duckling next to her toward which the hawk was driving. Her fat body struck against his hard, speed-driven talons. The hawk slashed angrily at her. Then as it realized it could not carry such a heavy burden into the air, swept upward. Scared and white-faced, Bill looked at the mother duck, lying on her side, moving feebly.

The terrified quacking of the ducklings excited Tonk and Tonka. They honked loudly. Mrs. Hopkins came running from the kitchen. She snatched off her apron and covered the mother duck. She had loved this foolish, friendly, fat bird. She had always felt such a pleasant sense of contentment as she watched her waddle importantly up and down the lane.

"Here, son," she said, and handed Bill the soft bundle, "take it back to the duck house and bury it. And bury the apron too." She shooed the bewildered ducklings toward their pen. Tonk and Tonka followed.

The sun was disappearing and the air was getting colder. This was the time of day when the mother duck spread her wings wide and covered the ducklings to keep them warm. If one fell from beneath this canopy of feathers it became chilled, and unless it could climb back, it died.

"Bill," his mother said, "go into your father's room and get a basket. We have to bring the ducklings into the kitchen and keep them warm. Hurry, and then you and Emmy can help me catch them."

The bewildered ducklings did not know what had happened to them. The cold wind made them shiver. It was time to nestle under protecting wings, but they could not find their mother.

As though she had decided something important, Tonka walked up to the little ducks. She quacked at them softly and turned toward a clump of bushes. She quatted down, still quacking. The ducklings followed her. Tonka lifted her wings gently. The ducklings scurried beneath them and Tonka folded her wings about their chilled bodies.

Tonka had adopted the ducklings. They stayed under her wings that night and for many nights thereafter. Now and then Tonk took her place. The ducklings grew fatter and bigger. People on Queen's Island still talk about Tonk and Tonka strutting up and down the dirt lane with a ragged procession of ducklings tumbling after them. Soon they were

leading their little charges into the yard that adjoined the terrace of the house. There, they learned, ground meal, peanut butter, bread dipped in milk, and the tender shoots that grew among the shrubbery, could be found.

Tonk and Tonka and the ducklings accepted one another as members of the same family. They fed side by side. The geese and the ducklings began following Emmy when she came from school. Once or twice she was even able to stroke Tonka's long neck.

IV

SPRING was everywhere on Queen's Island. The fishing boats were being scraped. The ocean and bays lost their cold green and became a soft blue. On Baffin Island the silent frozen land was again being warmed by the sun. Twilight had come, and soon the days would be endless. In far-off parts of the world, creatures of land, sea, and air felt the call to return to their nesting grounds.

Tonk and Tonka were becoming restless. More and more

often they swung into the air to spiral down on Tisman Pond or on the waters of the broad bay three miles away. The first question Bill and Emmy asked when they came home from school was: "Have they gone?"

Along the far-off Gulf of Mexico thousands of other blue geese were showing signs of restlessness as they winged their way from Louisiana and Texas to Vermilion Bay, which lies near the mouth of the Mississippi River. For days the blue geese came down, landing on the bay and its adjacent streams

and mud flats. They seemed to be everywhere — adrift on the water, moving about on the flats, digging out the roots of grasses. The air was dizzy with their excited cries. The blue geese have begun their journey north from this spot at exactly the same time every year, as long as man can remember.

Then, one morning, as the sun was sending out the rosy streamers of a new day, a great goose rose upward honking loudly. As he spiraled higher and higher into the sky, a ragged line of blue geese followed. With outstretched necks gleaming in the sun they began the long flight to Baffin Island.

On Queen's Island the hawks hatched their young. Day after day the male hawk scoured the countryside seeking food. The small birds fled or hid in deep-leaved trees. Quail crouched in the tall grass as the black shadow flew over them.

Daily now, Tonk and Tonka rose restlessly and disappeared. But they always came back at the first shadows of evening. At night Tonk would stand erect, head thrust upward, as if he were listening to some sound no one else could hear. He would honk loudly, ruffle his feathers, and spread his wings. Then his head would go down and he would sleep fitfully.

It was Saturday. On Thursday Tonk and Tonka had flown away and not returned. Mr. Hopkins, working in the yard, was certain that the geese had yielded to the call of spring and were headed north.

"I'd sure like to see them again," said Bill. Emmy, who was helping her mother prune some shrubbery, pointed to the sky. "There they come," she said calmly. "I knew they would."

High in the sky, like paper cutouts, Tonk and Tonka floated down, now beating their wings, now gliding on the air currents until they came to rest on the lane. Mrs. Hopkins, who had been watching happily, glanced into the duckyard.

"Look out!" she screamed. "The hawk. Chase it away."

Before anyone could move, the goshawk, diving at an angle was down among the ducklings and up again with a duckling struggling weakly against the sharp talons piercing its fat body.

Mr. Hopkins knew that there was nothing he could do but stand helplessly by. Then he shouted: "The geese, they're after the hawk!"

As the hawk rose, a little slowly because of the weight of the duckling in its claws, Tonk and Tonka sprang into the air.

Their necks were stretched to the utmost and their wings beat the air like flashes of bright color.

With his keen sight the hawk saw the geese rushing toward him. He flew sidewise, and then started to climb. Tonk flew upward. With mighty wingbeats he passed the hawk, while Tonka flying below cut off the downward path.

The goshawk tried to slide away from Tonk, but there was no escape. Tonk, his wings held stiff and motionless, shot straight down onto the hawk. There was a rush of wings, a clash of bodies, and then the tumbling mass of feathers separated. The duckling dropped from the hawk's talons and plummeted to earth.

The hawk came down heavily, turning over and over, until it landed in the field beyond the yard. Tonk and Tonka wheeled slowly in the air and honked in triumph. Then they flew higher in widening spirals and disappeared.

Mr. Hopkins leaped over the fence and picked up the dead hawk. Tonk had broken its back with his powerful wing. He had swooped downward and smashed his heavy wing bone into the hawk like a hammer, killing his enemy at once.

Hours later Tonk and Tonka landed near the duck house.

Mr. Hopkins wondered if they might, after all, settle down on the farm to hatch their young.

That night a storm blew out of the South and joined with the winds from the Middle West. The Weather Bureau warned that the winds would be of gale force and might reach sixty miles per hour. Small-craft warnings were issued, and everyone within the path of the storm was cautioned to fasten down anything that might be blown away.

Before he went to bed Mr. Hopkins put on his slicker and with Bill went out to have a final look around. As they came to the duck enclosure they heard, above the clashing tree branches and the roar of the wind, urgent honks coming from Tonk and Tonka. The geese were standing with heads erect, necks stretched out, in a state of great excitement. Between honks they stood rigid, listening.

As Bill and his father looked on, the tumbling clouds rolled back, and a dim moon peered through the night haze. Tonk and Tonka sprang into the air. They flew upward, honking all the way until they were out of sight. Father and son saw them again, for a moment, shadows against the moonlight. Then they were gone.

The blue geese which had left Vermilion Bay weeks before had been forced eastward by the spring gales. On this night they were passing over Queen's Island. As Tonk and Tonka flew out of the storm to join them, the leader honked a welcome.

On the island, Mr. Hopkins spoke softly: "A safe journey — and come back sometime."

006309554

CL STACKS

J Ackerman   c.2
    Tonk and Tonka.

CHILDREN'S LIBRARY

DETROIT PUBLIC LIBRARY

The number of books that may be
drawn at one time by the card holder
is governed by the reasonable needs of
the reader and the material on hand.

Books for junior readers are subject
to special rules.